1/08

04/2013
2
10/2010

Incarceration Issues:
Punishment, Reform, and Rehabilitation

TITLE LIST

YOUTH IN PRISON

by Roger Smith
and Marsha McIntosh

Mason Crest Publishers
Philadelphia

Mason Crest Publishers Inc.
370 Reed Road
Broomall, Pennsylvania 19008
(866) MCP-BOOK (toll free)

3 4 5 6 7 8 9 10

Library of Congress Cataloging-in-Publication Data

Smith, Roger, 1959 Aug. 15–
  Youth in prison / by Roger Smith and Marsha McIntosh.
     p. cm. — (Incarceration issues)
  Includes index.
  ISBN 1-59084-990-6   ISBN 1-59084-984-1 (series)
  ISBN 978-1-59084-990-3   ISBN 978-1-59084-984-2 (series)

  1. Juvenile justice, Administration of—Juvenile literature. 2. Juvenile detention—United States—Juvenile literature. 3. Juvenile detention—Canada—Juvenile literature. I. McIntosh, Marsha. II. Title. III. Series.
  HV9069.S65 2007
  365'.420973—dc22
                          2006002233

Interior design by MK Bassett-Harvey.
Interiors produced by Harding House Publishing Service, Inc.
www.hardinghousepages.com

Cover design by Peter Spires Culotta.

Printed in Malaysia by Times Offset (M) Sdn.Bhd.

Contents

INTRODUCTION

by Larry E. Sullivan, Ph.D.

Prisons will be with us as long as we have social enemies. We will punish them for acts that we consider criminal, and we will confine them in institutions.

Prisons have a long history, one that fits very nicely in the religious context of sin, evil, guilt, and expiation. In fact, the motto of one of the first prison reform organizations was "Sin no more." Placing offenders in prison was, for most of the history of the prison, a ritual for redemption through incarceration; hence the language of punishment takes on a very theological cast. The word "penitentiary" itself comes from the religious concept of penance. When we discuss prisons, we are dealing not only with the law but with very strong emotions and reactions to acts that range from minor or misdemeanor crimes to major felonies like murder and rape.

Prisons also reflect the level of the civilizing process through which a culture travels, and it tells us much about how we treat our fellow human beings. The great nineteenth-century Russian author Fyodor Dostoyevsky, who was a political prisoner, remarked, "The degree of civilization in a society can be measured by observing its prisoners." Similarly, Winston Churchill, the great British prime minister during World War II, said that the "treatment of crime and criminals is one of the most unfailing tests of civilization of any country."

Since the very beginnings of the American Republic, we have attempted to improve and reform the way we imprison criminals. For much of the history of the American prison, we tried to rehabilitate or modify the criminal behavior of offenders through a variety of treatment programs. In the last quarter of the twentieth century, politicians and citizens alike realized that this attempt had failed, and we began passing stricter laws, imprisoning people for longer terms and building more prisons. This movement has taken a great toll on society. Approximately two million people are behind bars today. This movement has led to the

YOUTH IN PRISON

overcrowding of prisons, worse living conditions, fewer educational programs, and severe budgetary problems. There is also a significant social cost, since imprisonment splits families and contributes to a cycle of crime, violence, drug addiction, and poverty.

All these are reasons why this series on incarceration issues is extremely important for understanding the history and culture of the United States. Readers will learn all facets of punishment: its history; the attempts to rehabilitate offenders; the increasing number of women and juveniles in prison; the inequality of sentencing among the races; attempts to find alternatives to incarceration; the high cost, both economically and morally, of imprisonment; and other equally important issues. These books teach us the importance of understanding that the prison system affects more people in the United States than any institution, other than our schools.

CHAPTER 1.

A Brief History of Juvenile Justice

Elizabeth Fry's friends begged her not to go. The prison had a terrible reputation: female prisoners would rip the clothes off visitors' backs, take any valuables, and hurl verbal abuse. It was 1812, and though Newgate Prison was one of the most *infamous* of its day, Elizabeth was not put off by her friends' fears. A deeply religious *Quaker*, she felt compelled to go. "Hath not the Lord commanded us to remember those in prison?" she asked. So she entered Newgate, refusing even to take off her watch.

Nothing could have prepared Elizabeth for what she saw. Hundreds of drunken women dressed in rags were crammed into four crowded rooms, prostitutes, thieves, and innocent people together, all waiting for their trials. Children whose only crime was that they had nowhere else to go were mixed in with the adults.

Elizabeth Fry got to work, and spent the rest of her life diligently working to better the lives of Newgate's inmates. The prison became so extraordinary that world leaders heard of it and came to consult with her. Elizabeth became a ***philanthropist*** known for her prison and social reforms.

Until the twentieth century, societies judged juvenile offenders the same way they judged adult offenders. In Canada and the United States, as in much of the world, society viewed children as little adults. Punishments were very harsh for youths who committed crimes; many minor crimes were even punishable by death. It was not until the nineteenth century that attitudes began to change and soften as people began to realize that children had special needs. In the 150 years since then, there have been many important changes in juvenile incarceration.

THE CANADIAN JUVENILE JUSTICE SYSTEM

According to the Department of Justice Canada (DJC) Web site, the first effort in Canada to separate juvenile offenders from adult criminals occurred in 1858 when two reformatories were established on the Georgian Bay. One reformatory was at Isle-aux-Noix on the Richelieu River to serve eastern Canada; one at Penetanguishene served western Canada.

Both institutions had problems from the beginning. The facilities were old army barracks dating from the War of 1812, and authorities allowed too large of an age range of youths (up to age twenty-four) to be incarcerated in the institutions. There were no training programs, no discipline, and many escapes. Both centers ran on the principles of work and

In the early nineteenth century, Elizabeth Fry worked hard to improve prison conditions.

This early juvenile reformatory was in Rochester, New York.

punishment instead of **rehabilitation**, so the institutions did nothing to educate or reform youths.

Juvenile offenders were also held under horrendous conditions at jails. An inspector reported in 1865 of a Montreal jail, "One is horror stricken at seeing little boys in rags and older offenders in almost a state of nudity, commingling together, with matted hair and countenances bedaubed with filth." Information like this urged reformers to make changes, and they began to win victories for the cause of juvenile justice.

A member of the board of inspectors of asylums and prisons, E. A. Meredith, reported in 1862 that imprisoning youths in jails was the total ruin of them. In his opinion, jails were "nurseries of vice and hotbeds of crime," so Meredith began encouraging the system to place neglected children in youth reformatories to help in the prevention of delinquency. He encouraged reformatories to be places where proper care, training in a trade, and education be given. Prevention was a better way to go, Meredith believed, because it was "more agreeable, more hopeful, more economical, more humane, and more socially responsible."

In 1864, a group opened the Halifax Protestant Industrial School. The purpose of the school was to give a home, technical training, and education to homeless and neglected boys on the streets. Although the school's goal was to *prevent* juvenile delinquents, the state began sending boys convicted of crimes for rehabilitation. Volunteers ran the school, and the

Only boys were sent to reformatories like this one, where most of them endured horrendous conditions.

atmosphere was homey, clean, and safe. Discipline was not severe, and the boys had so much freedom they could even leave if they chose. Unfortunately, the school lacked money and had trouble running good programs and getting good staff. The boys often took jobs in town to help the school, and they did most of the maintenance work around the school.

The Halifax school was the beginning of new ideas for juvenile delinquent care across Canada. A middle- and upper-class group called the

The Halifax Protestant Industrial School took in "wayward" boys and educated them in a trade.

Child Savers also started promoting new approaches. They helped start free public school education, industrial schools, new progressive laws, and foster-family care.

The industrial school movement began in Ontario in 1887. These schools emphasized character development, moral training, education, and vocational training. By the end of the 1880s, there were seven schools for boys and girls in the province of Quebec that were some of the best reformatory schools in Canada. At the same time, the Brothers of Charity ran one of the best schools in Montreal, where the Catholic brothers, acting as counselors and teachers, worked side by side with the boys. This school placed great importance on the development of a trade so the boys would be able to support themselves as adults. The school's leather products had an excellent reputation.

By 1890, Canada had special courts for juveniles, qualified staff for juvenile schools, limited detention for youths under age fourteen, and indefinite sentences. (If a youth showed great improvement in moral character, he was released before his sentence was completed.)

By the early 1900s, reformers became convinced that many juvenile delinquents were often the victims of crime instead of the cause of crime. Studies had shown that most troubled youth came from poor circumstances with family problems or neglectful parents. Reformers started pushing for more understanding and social treatment for these youths. Some Canadians disagreed, saying society should not coddle delinquents but should give them tough consequences. Reformers won a victory in 1908 with the passage of Juvenile Delinquents Act. It stated that "every juvenile delinquent shall be treated, not as a criminal, but as a misguided and misdirected child." Juvenile courts were established in which all youths were tried. However, any youth over the age of fourteen who committed serious crimes such as murder was tried in an adult court. This act set the tone for juvenile justice in Canada for almost seventy-five years.

In the 1960s, more reforms improved juvenile facilities. In 1984, the Young Offenders Act was passed, replacing the 1908 Juvenile Delinquents Act. The new law addressed the offender's rights more than the previous act had, and it also tried to make youths more accountable for their actions. The new act had a more **benevolent** attitude toward delinquents, but also lowered the age for prosecution to age twelve and the maximum age the law would apply to seventeen. In 2003, another law, the Youth Criminal Justice Act was enacted with the intention of remedying the faults of the Young Offenders Act of 1984. One of its goals is to reduce the use of juvenile incarceration and work more on placing offenders back into the community after custody.

A BRIEF HISTORY OF JUVENILE JUSTICE

In the 1800s, children worked in textile factories, as well as many other industries.

HISTORY OF THE UNITED STATES JUVENILE JUSTICE SYSTEM

Prior to the nineteenth century, U.S. society seemed to understand the concept of infants and toddlers but had no understanding of childhood and its special needs. When children got into trouble and their families could not handle them, society punished them in one of three ways: authorities bound them to middle- and upper-class skilled artisans as ***apprentices***; children were bound to any responsible adult to be used in any way the adult needed; or churches administered discipline such as whippings, beatings, or brandings, the same punishments that any adult would receive.

When the Industrial Revolution began in the 1800s, factory life replaced the family in the lives of many poor children. Children often left home at an early age and traveled around the country looking for work in factories. Many social problems such as child crime, drunkenness, and *vagrancy* worsened during this time, and mass immigration caused similar problems.

Early reformers interested in rehabilitating rather than punishing youth offenders built the New York House of Refuge in 1824. Its main purpose was to reform poor *wayward* children and help them become productive members of society. Individual states also began to see the problems of juvenile incarceration and began building similar youth reform homes that were like orphanages. Many of the youth in these homes were orphans and homeless. The state took on the responsibility of parenting youth offenders until they showed a positive change in their behavior, or until they became adults.

In the 1830s, the practice of "placing out" began as authorities sent problem children to farms in the Midwest and West to work. Some families treated the children as family members, but many abused them and made them work rigorously as farmhands.

In the late 1800s, after the Civil War, reform schools, industrial schools, or training schools housed the many vagrant children roaming the country. The word "school" was used loosely; these were mostly just holding pens for the children. The cottage reformatories had fewer children (twenty to forty) with adult role models living with them, but the institutional reformatories held as many as five hundred children in a cell block. Though children received a formal education that was very *moralistic*, they did not usually learn a trade.

In the late 1800s, women, including Jane Addams, Lucy Flower, and Julia Lathrop, convinced state legislatures to create a separate justice system for children. Due mostly to their efforts, on July 3, 1899, the first juvenile court in the United States began on the west side of Chicago, Illinois. The youth courts were more informal than the adult version, with the judges considering any *extenuating* circumstances relating to the crime

Jane Addams helped convince state legislators to create a separate justice system for children.

or behavior, not just the bare facts. By 1925, all but two states had juvenile courts, most following the Chicago model that included a judge who only presided over juveniles, informal hearings held in offices instead of courtrooms, and cases closed to the public. These juvenile courts kept records that were sealed when the children reached age eighteen, and whenever possible, probation was used as the main punishment.

In the 1960s and early 1970s, some important changes were made to create a more just juvenile court system. Youth courts were very different from adult courts; there was no jury and often no lawyer. Juveniles did not have the rights provided for under the Fifth and Fourteenth amendments. (The Fifth Amendment gives the right to a trial by jury and the freedom from *self-incrimination*, and the Fourteenth Amendment gives all citizens equal protection under the law.)

Congress passed the Juvenile Delinquency Prevention and Control Act in 1968. This law encouraged communities to plan programs to help control delinquency at the local level. In 1974, lawmakers passed the Juvenile Justice and Delinquency Prevention Act, which created three new groups: the Office of Juvenile Justice and Delinquency Prevention (OJJDP), the National Institute for Juvenile Justice and Delinquency Prevention (NIJJDP), and the Runaway Youth Program. If states wanted to receive funding provided for in this law, they had to move all juveniles from secure detention facilities and separate them from adult criminals. Evidence had proven that juveniles were learning worse criminal behavior from these older inmates.

Between 1980 and the mid-1990s, crime rose sharply in the United States, peaked in 1994, and then slowly declined. Legislatures, afraid the increase in the 1980s would continue, cracked down on offenders with a "get tough on crime" attitude. Lawmakers amended the Juvenile Justice Act of 1974 to allow youths who committed certain violent crimes and violated weapons laws to be tried as adults. This new attitude of toughness brought about changes in the juvenile system so that it became more like the adult criminal courts. Instead of seeing delinquents as "youth begging rehabilitation," society now saw them as criminals, and rehabilitation was no longer a priority.

A BRIEF HISTORY OF JUVENILE JUSTICE

TIME TO RETHINK

Time spent in detention can be valuable for juveniles, a chance to stop and think about the reasons for their crimes. What are the forces running their lives? Will this be the first and last time, or is this just the beginning of a criminal career? Detention gives a juvenile a chance to be away from violent streets, unhealthy peer pressure, and chaotic families.

In the late 1990s, against a background of school shootings and other heinous crimes, the public began to fear a new breed of juvenile offenders. The OJJDP called them "juvenile superpredators" and "juveniles for whom violence was a way of life—new delinquents unlike youth of past generations." Later, in February 2000, the OJJDP wrote in their *Juvenile Justice Bulletin* that this threat of juvenile violence had been greatly exaggerated, but fear at that time caused some major changes in the juvenile justice system.

According to the United States 1999 Annual Report of the Coalition for Juvenile Justice, "Contrary to popular belief, fewer than one third of youth in detention facilities are being held for violent offenses—assaults, rapes, murders and robberies—that dominate the headlines." Most incarcerated youths are held for drug offenses, property crimes, and technical violations of the law. Many are there for status offenses such as running away from home or being "unmanageable."

In the United States, the average time in juvenile detention is two weeks, though many youths pass through a detention center in just a few hours while others stay for months waiting on court action. In Canada, in 1997, 50 percent of the sentences given to juveniles were for one to three months, 25 percent were for less than one month, and officials sentenced 8 percent for more than six months.

Youth have always gotten in trouble. How youthful offenders are handled, however, has changed as society has changed. The way North Americans define crime, rehabilitation, and adolescence itself all shape what happens when juveniles break the law.

CHAPTER 2

The Juvenile Justice System

Jabakki Granderson was only fifteen years old in 1994 when he was arrested and convicted of murdering a man. In Susan Kilbourne's book *Children Behind Bars: Youth Who Are Detained, Incarcerated and Executed,* she tells the story of how Granderson was rehabilitated and the relationship he formed with the judge who presided over his trial. While in detention, Granderson began writing Judge Yvette McGee Brown: "He wanted her to know that he was not 'who she saw in the courtroom or what it said on paper.'" Granderson told her he had started to understand how much he wronged his victim's family and those who knew him. He knew his mother raised him to live a

better life than he had lived up to this point. When Granderson completed an internship program in printing technology and earned his high school diploma along with his printing technology certificate, he let the judge know. "She wrote back, which I really didn't expect, but she's got a really huge heart. Thank God she did write me back every time," Granderson later said of the judge.

Because he had no prior record, Judge Yvette McGee Brown denied a motion to transfer Granderson to an adult court when he first appeared before her. Later, after he had served six to eight months, she was impressed when he wrote her a letter confessing he had not been honest with her in court. In his testimony, he had claimed the murder was in self-defense, but in reality, it was about drugs. He did not ask for anything; he just wanted to clear his conscience. After that, he wrote to her every four or five months to tell her what he was accomplishing. "When he wrote me the letter asking if he could be considered for early release, I granted the hearing."

The judge was pleased that Granderson's social worker came with him to the hearing, because this was something that hardly ever happens. The social worker told the judge how much Granderson had accomplished during his incarceration, including the fact that he had become a leader and role model to the other youths. The social worker was concerned about the message it would send other youths if, after all Granderson's accomplishments, he was denied early release. For the first time in her career, Judge Yvette McGee Brown granted an early release to a youth **adjudicated** on murder. Granderson had convinced her that he had been rehabilitated.

STEPS IN THE UNITED STATES JUVENILE JUSTICE SYSTEM

A juvenile enters the justice system when a parent, agency, citizen, or police report an offense to the juvenile court. The court intake officer eval-

There are important differences in the language used in juvenile courts and adult courts. Juveniles are not "convicted," they are "adjudicated." They are not "arrested," they go through "intake." Intake is also a procedure between the child, parents, social worker, and a police officer to decide if authorities should handle the case informally or formally. A "delinquency proceeding" is a court action to declare someone a juvenile delinquent. A "delinquent" is someone under the age of eighteen whom a judge adjudicates in juvenile court of something that would be a crime if committed by an adult. A "status offense" is an activity that is illegal for a minor to do but not for an adult such as running away, skipping school, violations of curfew, or always disobeying parents.

uates the case and decides if the youth should be referred to a social service agency or if the case should be heard in juvenile court.

If the case is serious, authorities will keep the youth in a detention facility, shelter, group home, or foster home; juvenile offenders are not released on bail. If the intake officer decides the youth does not need to go to juvenile court, he will decide if mental health services, counseling from school counselors, or help from other youth service agencies is necessary. The decision is based on several factors: the seriousness of the crime, the attitude and remorse level of the juvenile, and any history of delinquency.

If the intake officer decides the youth should have a formal court hearing, he sends a petition to the juvenile court. The petition lists the laws the youth allegedly has broken. If the crime is serious, such as rape or murder, officials may refer the case to the district attorney's office, and

A runaway is considered a status offender.

the youth may be tried as an adult. If the case goes to a juvenile court and the youth admits to the charges, the judge may order a treatment program. If the youth denies the allegations, then she will have a court hearing much like an adult would.

If the judge charges the juvenile guilty, he may rule she is delinquent or a status offender. A second court hearing is scheduled to determine whether the juvenile will be put on probation (if she has committed a nonserious crime) or whether she will be placed in a juvenile correctional facility. The judge may give another treatment option such as **community service** or making **restitution** to the victim. Some judges send juveniles to a group home or work camp in hopes of rehabilitating them. Other times, judges may allow youths to stay at home and receive special social services.

After serving time in a detention center, authorities will either directly release the youth or place him on "aftercare," a type of **parole**. Placement in a **halfway house** is another release option. Here, youth are under twenty-four-hour supervision. When the youth has finished with parole or aftercare, she is released from the system.

DELINQUENTS, STATUS OFFENDERS, AND ABANDONED YOUTH

According to Thomas O'Connor, an expert in juvenile justice, the U.S. juvenile justice system has approximately 4,000 courts. The system's goal is to rehabilitate problem youth and to consider even the worst offender—the delinquent—a mistaken or sick child rather than a criminal or bad person. The courts sentence 54 percent to probation, 28 percent to detention, 13 percent with a fine, and 5 percent with a conditional release. The courts process approximately 1.8 million delinquents a year.

A status offender is a juvenile caught doing something that is illegal for a youth but not for an adult. These offenses include running away

In some states, a juvenile arrested for a serious crime can be tried as an adult.

from home, missing school (truant), and being unmanageable; there are approximately 2.2 million status offenders each year. The police usually send them to a system of group homes and shelters, and they are put into one of several programs: PINS—person in need of supervision, CHIPS—children in need of protection and services, or MINS—minors in need of supervision by the courts or a child protective agency.

Youth who have committed offenses are not the only ones for whom the juvenile justice system is responsible. The justice system is also responsible for children who are without proper parental supervision. O'Conner reports that almost one million children are left alone by their parents each year, and 750,000 are abandoned. On average, 125 infants are left in public places each year, and 400 are orphaned because their parents die. Unclaimed babies at hospitals number 31,000, and 600 are left for dead in attempted **infanticides**. The courts send these children to a system of state homes for boys and girls, orphanages, and private foundation homes.

Abused and neglected children form another group of children that are under the care of the juvenile justice system. Each year, authorities report approximately 3.3 million of these cases to the state. One-third of these are confirmed cases that officials put into foster-home placements.

Different states deal with these problems in different ways. One of the biggest variations is the age at which the state says a person is an adult. In thirty-nine states, the age is eighteen years old. Eight states—Texas, Louisiana, Georgia, South Carolina, Georgia, Illinois, Missouri, Michigan, and Massachusetts—set the age at seventeen. New York, North Carolina, and Connecticut set the age of *majority* at sixteen. When a youth reaches the age of majority, officials try them in an adult court.

JUVENILE COURT OR ADULT COURT?

In the United States, states also differ in the types of cases tried in a juvenile court. Some states are *exclusive*—they will only try minor crimes or status offenses in a juvenile court, while serious crimes such as murder or rape are tried in an adult court. In other states, the courts must hear all cases involving juveniles in the juvenile courts first, regardless of the crime. Some states hear the case in the juvenile courts and the adult court at the same time. As might be expected, punishments are usually harsher when a juvenile is convicted as an adult.

THE CANADIAN JUVENILE JUSTICE SYSTEM

The Youth Criminal Justice Act gives several options to the police and the Crown on how to proceed when authorities suspect a young person of committing a crime. If authorities take *extrajudicial* measures, they will

not prosecute the youth in a court but will still hold the youth accountable for their actions. The youth will have to make amends to the victim. Officials use this tactic with first-time, nonviolent offenders. According to the Department of Justice Canada Web site, when authorities take extrajudicial measures:

- The police may decide if further action is necessary.

- The police may warn the youth of the potential for charging him with the crime and the consequences of his actions but take no further action.

- The police may have the parents of the youth meet at the police station for a meeting and caution both parties.

- The police may, with the youth's permission, enroll her in a community program that will help her stay away from crime.

- The Crown may write a letter to the parents about the crime, telling them of the consequences should it happen again.

ALTERNATIVE SENTENCING IN CANADA

Many people in Canada have pushed for alternative sentencing. They believe that putting a juvenile in a detention center is not always the best way to rehabilitate him. The story of Kevin Hollinsky, as told on the Church Council on Justice and Corrections Web site, illustrates this point.

One night in 1994, Kevin and four friends spent a night out on the town at a bar. Several hours later, they got into Kevin's car to return home. While on the road, Kevin tried to get the attention of a car full of girls. He was going too fast and lost control of the car. The accident killed two of his close friends and injured the other two. The Crown asked for a jail term for Kevin, but because of a resourceful judge and the interven-

Drunken driving can lead to serious consequences.

tion of the parents of the boys who died, the court gave him an alternative sentence instead.

Kevin spent 750 hours of community service traveling to schools with the extremely damaged car he drove on that fateful evening. He spoke of the consequences of irresponsibility, and students saw firsthand the mangled car. Some Canadians were opposed to the alternative sentence,

Juvenile offenders often deserve a second chance.

thinking that Kevin was getting off too easily, but, Lloyd Grahame, a retired police staff sergeant commented, "I've got to say now that he makes the case for alternative sentencing. . . . You could send him to jail for five years and you wouldn't have punished him like you punished him by doing what happened here. This man was forced to live with his irresponsibility day after day."

Kevin was a living object lesson to 8,200 high school students in his region. The presentation affected students profoundly: for the first time, that summer the region had no fatal or serious accidents involving high school students. Kevin's punishment was far more meaningful and inexpensive than if he had gone to prison. Kevin suffered **survivor guilt** and **posttraumatic stress disorder**, making his sentence even more difficult for him. At the same time, however, Kevin's sentence allowed him to do something concrete to make amends for his crime.

For some juvenile offenders, like Kevin Hollinsky, alternative programs are the most effective ways to deal with their crimes. There are others, however, for whom incarceration seems to be the better answer.

CHAPTER 3

WHY ARE JUVENILES INCARCERATED?

Mitch came from a troubled, middle-class white family. His father and mother divorced when he was a baby, and he had constant conflict with his stepfather, his mother's fourth husband. According to *Youth in Prison*, by M. A. Bortner and Linda M. Williams, authorities referred him to juvenile court at age thirteen for giving a false report to police. He ran away from home four times. He and his family attended counseling sessions after his stepfather accused him of stealing money and weapons from him. One weekend, Mitch's parents left him home alone. His thirteen-year-old girlfriend came over, and while playing a game, Mitch pointed his stepfather's gun

at her head and pulled the trigger. The gun went off, the girl died, and Mitch fled the scene. Using one of his mother's credit cards, he bought an airline ticket and flew to an uncle's house in another state. A few days later, the police picked him up and brought him back to his hometown.

Mitch told the police that he had accidentally shot his friend, became scared, and ran. At first, investigators said that it had been an "unintentional discharge." A neighbor had good things to say about Mitch: he felt that the incident was just bad judgment. The father of the girlfriend felt that Mitch was a normal, friendly person and felt sorry that Mitch would have to live with the tragedy for the rest of his life. The girlfriend's father was very upset with Mitch's parents for leaving guns available in the house while they were away.

Those involved with the case were alarmed when the prosecution charged Mitch with first- and second-degree homicide. Some citizens called the police and expressed their anger at the charge. The victim's father was surprised authorities charged a thirteen-year-old so harshly. Mitch stood trial in a juvenile court and pleaded guilty to the charge. He was sentenced to a juvenile detention center.

Tomás, a Mexican American, ran away from home five times after the age of thirteen. According to *Youth in Prison*, he had a difficult home life. When Tomás was three, his father left the family, and he never had any contact with him. His mother had a boyfriend who abused drugs and alcohol; this man also physically abused Tomás's mother and his sisters and brothers. Tomás saw the boyfriend as an "intruder" and was very angry with his own father for abandoning the family.

When Tomás was thirteen, he lived on the streets for three months, and his mother made no real effort to find him. That same year, the court charged him with theft and put him on **probation**. The court extended his probation twice for violations and other theft charges. When Tomás was fifteen, he fought against his mother's abusive boyfriend. Authorities referred him to the court for domestic violence but dismissed the charges. Finally, at the age of sixteen, Tomás was sent to court for burglary. The judge adjudicated him and sent him to a detention center.

Life on the streets often leads to crime and legal offenses.

Authors Bortner and Williams also describe Daniel, an African American boy who lived with his mother. His father lived in the Midwest and had no contact with his son. Daniel resented his new stepfather and went to live with his uncle. He missed so much school he was suspended. School records showed he used marijuana, alcohol, and crack. Then Daniel joined a gang, and began to cruise rival neighborhoods, looking to start trouble. One time they did a drive-by at twelve o'clock in the afternoon, and they shot and killed members of another gang who had jumped one of their homeboys (members).

Daniel believed that his gang had some values. For instance, they did not kill babies. Anyone four and under was considered a baby, but if a child was as old as eight, they were old enough to be a ***gang-banger***. Whenever his gang had a "job" to do, they would smoke a "shiner," something like angel dust or PCP that would slow down their hearts and make them very strong. If they were shot, Daniel said, "It's like you're already dead, so you won't feel it." One of his homeboys was shot, seemed to be dead, but revived and earned the nickname, O. G. Black Lazarus.

Gangs often have a negative influence on urban youth.

DANIEL ON JOINING A GANG:

If you don't got a family, best you gonna go to a gang, because they're just like a family. . . . Some people join because they been getting child abuse or sexual abuse or something. . . . When people got problems with their family, and they don't want to go live with their mom some-where—they got to get on the streets and then learn to work the streets and all of a sudden they're gonna try to get in the gang.

—from *Youth in Prison* by M. A. Bortner and Linda M. Williams

Daniel was almost seventeen before police arrested him for the first time. The court adjudicated him of aggravated assault and sentenced him to a youth prison. His victim had been a rival gang member, a young pregnant woman whom he said had, "disrespected his hood."

Once upon a time there were two friends; we'll call them Stacey and Amanda. They liked to do the same sorts of things; they laughed at the same jokes; they got the same grades in school; and they even looked a lot alike. But Stacey came from an alcoholic family where she did not receive much encouragement, while Amanda was close to her parents. Stacey's home was filled with verbal and even physical violence; Amanda's home, on the other hand, was the place where she felt most comfortable, the place where she could always count on being understood and supported. Amanda cried for Stacey when she came to school with bruises where her father had hit her. The two girls cried together when

Few youthful offenders are under age twelve.

HOW OLD ARE JUVENILE OFFENDERS?

Juvenile offenders under the age of twelve are very unusual. Most incarcerated youths are age fifteen and older.

someone stabbed Stacey's brother. They were still good friends—but Amanda couldn't imagine what Stacey's life was like.

In high school, Stacey started to get in trouble, and the court put her into group homes. Eventually, Stacey committed a murder, and authorities placed her in a youth facility. Meanwhile, Amanda is in college. These two friends had much in common—but not their family lives. That difference led them down two very separate paths. A troubled family life seems to be one common denominator among juvenile offenders.

"IN THE CONTEXT OF THEIR LIVES"

Authors Bortner and Williams believe that it is necessary to place, "youths' delinquent behavior and their imprisonment in the contexts of their lives. . . . [Juvenile offenders'] experiences, problems, and potentials are inseparable from their life circumstances and positions within society."

Although each youth in detention is an individual, most are between fifteen and seventeen years old, and in the United States, most juveniles in detention centers are from a minority. In Arizona, for example, Latinos (mostly Mexican Americans) make up 44 percent of incarcerated

In Canada, more Aboriginal youths are incarcerated than non-Aboriginal.

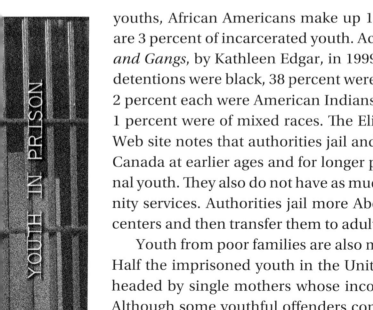
youths, African Americans make up 15 percent, and American Indians are 3 percent of incarcerated youth. According to *Youth Violence, Crime, and Gangs*, by Kathleen Edgar, in 1999, 39 percent of youths in juvenile detentions were black, 38 percent were white, 18 percent were Hispanic, 2 percent each were American Indians and Asian/Pacific Islanders, and 1 percent were of mixed races. The Elizabeth Fry Society of Manitoba's Web site notes that authorities jail and criminalize **Aboriginal** youth in Canada at earlier ages and for longer periods of time than non-Aboriginal youth. They also do not have as much access to a lawyer and community services. Authorities jail more Aboriginal youth offenders in youth centers and then transfer them to adult jails.

Youth from poor families are also more likely to end up in detention. Half the imprisoned youth in the United States come from households headed by single mothers whose incomes are below the poverty level. Although some youthful offenders come from middle- and upper-class families, an overwhelming majority live in poor circumstances. Poverty

Forty-four percent of all incarcerated youths are Latino.

produces social isolation and economic distress. It undermines the relevance of school. It fosters despair, disorganization, and social deterioration, all conditions that produce crime.

Age and gender make a difference in delinquent activity as well. Although male and female juveniles are nearly equal in number, in the United States, authorities incarcerate many more males than females. In 1999, according to the Census of Juveniles in Residential Placement (CJRP), 86.6 percent of juvenile offenders were male, and 13.4 percent were female. There are many theories as to why more males commit crimes than females. In the neighborhoods where most juvenile delinquents come from, males express themselves by being aggressive, having control, and having sexual ability. Conflict is normal, and male youths admire the dominant person.

The Public Safety and Emergency Preparedness Canada Web site says that criminality in the family is the strongest pull on a child toward delinquent behavior. If an older member of the family is a convicted criminal, a child is two times more likely to be involved in delinquency. Other family characteristics can help point a child toward delinquency, including factors such as parental neglect (unsupervised children, no parental involvement), disruptions (divorce, absent parents, sick parents), parental characteristics (alcoholism, immaturity, violence), and conflict (inconsistent discipline, parent–child rejection).

RACE, GENDER, AND CLASS

Authors Bortner and Williams explore what it means to be a minority, male, and poor. Many times, these young people lack adequate housing, medical and dental care, clothing, food, and education. Families with higher incomes are able to provide their children with these things, but poorer families often go without many necessities. Authorities have made many cuts in the funding of youth social programs that formerly helped enhance communities' and families' sparse incomes. Worry about the poverty that engulfs their families is a problem for these young people. Many feel responsible for their mothers and younger brothers and sis-

Researchers in Quebec, Canada, found that out of 400 students studied, children from the poorest families had the highest incidents of violence. Five percent of very poor girls were violent, whereas 1 percent of girls from rich families showed violent behavior. Fourteen percent of boys from poor families exhibited violence, whereas 5 percent of wealthy boys had violent behavior. When families in poverty are lacking necessities, it takes the parents' attention away from the care of their children. These children usually have many problems and many times commit crimes later in life.

Source: Public Safety and Emergency Preparedness Canada Web site

ters, but jobs are hard to find. This increases their feelings of hopelessness and fear. Some adults in their neighborhoods have worked for years at minimum-wage jobs with nothing to show for their hard work, and youths see generations of adults living their entire lives on welfare. When children grow up with these role models, it is not a surprise that some of them express contempt for "straight jobs."

Of course, not all minority poor juveniles become involved in delinquent activities. Thousands live straight lives outside of prison. The reasons why some end up in juvenile detention centers are many. Self-image, identity, and socialization play a large part.

A WORLD OF PROBLEMS

Most young offenders have had problems long before their first induction into the juvenile justice system. Many delinquents experience

Children who experience abuse are more apt to be incarcerated when they are older.

issues of emotional and severe psychological disorders, abuse and ne-glect, and special education needs. Early on, troubles in school may leave them branded as "disruptive." They have often been diagnosed as being emotionally handicapped, learning disabled, or just "not normal." Bort-ner and Williams found that numerous juvenile offenders had come to believe they were inferior to other students who were successful in the classroom. Some of them quit coming to school, and some reacted with hostility and defiance.

The Department of Justice Canada Web site reports that many troubled juveniles have shown aggressive, disruptive, and antisocial behavior since early childhood. The majority of these youths come from troubled homes. It is common for delinquent youths in both the United States and Canada to have experienced sexual, emotional, or physical abuse. U.S. case files are filled with stories of beatings from family members who used hangers, water hoses, fists, belts, and extension cords. In one case, child protective services came to a single youth's home twenty times in fourteen years. Youths inside a model prison discussed in Bortner and Williams' book say that most people on the outside of their communities do not understand what they face in their neighborhoods. Their everyday realities include fear and death. They may kill or be killed, and weapons of various sorts are easily obtained.

In poorer neighborhoods, many families have one parent who is incarcerated. In Canada, 25,000 children have mothers in prison. According to Voices for Children Web site, these children are at high risk for criminal behavior. Most of them live in poverty and do not have adequate supervision. Other students sometimes ***stigmatize*** them at school, and they experience shame. Sometimes they develop harmful coping strategies such as turning to drugs and alcohol. Often children rationalize their mother's behavior as being necessary. Some may feel that going to prison is part of their family heritage, an attitude that in turn encourages their own antisocial actions. Many adolescents of incarcerated adults end up in the juvenile detention system.

Race prejudice can also influence a teen's identity. A Mexican American youth in an Arizona detention center told authors Bortner and Williams that when a police officer sees a group of his friends hanging out on the street, the officer would automatically think they are a gang: "You can be walkin' down the street, they'll stop you. . . . They look at you like that—like they automatically assume that you're guilty of something by the way you look."

Young adults whose parents have been involved in criminal activities are more apt to break the law themselves.

Young adults with mothers in prison are more apt to turn to alcohol as a coping strategy.

Many incarcerated youth share the same common experiences. They are bound by a history of physical and emotional abuse; their lives have been filled with terrible boredom, poor school experiences, and poverty. Such experiences affect how people see themselves, how they make sense of the world, and how they view their place in it.

CRIMES THAT DON'T PAY

A common myth about juveniles is that imprisoned youth are mostly dangerous and violent. Most crimes committed by Canadian youth are nonviolent property crimes; approximately half of these charges are for theft of under $5,000. In the United States, according to the FBI, in 2002,

Most juvenile offenders have committed nonviolent property crimes, such as breaking windows.

In Bortner and Williams' book, a teen describes his drug usage:

"I was high twenty-four hours a day. I'm sayin' the truth . . . the first thing people wake up they go to the restroom, wash their face, brush their teeth. Well, I'd do that, but I'd wake up, you know, light up a joint. . . . It's like a sickness."

there were 447,048 arrests for violent crimes such as murder, robbery, rape, and aggravated assault. The report showed that 1,170,165 arrests were made for property crimes, which are offenses of motor vehicle theft, burglary, *larceny*-theft, and *arson*. Of the juveniles in a model program discussed by Bortner and Williams, police arrested 138 of the 385 youths for violent crimes. Authorities incarcerated the others for crimes of property *felonies*, drug offenses, and *misdemeanors*. The youths involved in the project were a reflection of the general incarcerated juvenile population.

The use of drugs and alcohol is rampant among incarcerated youth. Many have used alcohol and drugs as early as age eight. Some started abusing these substances at home, others on the street.

Before becoming part of the juvenile justice system, many juvenile offenders had few if any people to whom they had to account for their actions. Once entering a detention facility, that changes—drastically.

CHAPTER 4

A Day in Juvenile Detention

Clallam County Detention Facility, located in Port Angeles, Washington, is not unlike most other detention centers. The experiences of a new "resident" are comparable to those in facilities all over the country.

A police escort usually brings the juvenile to the detention facility. When the police car arrives, the control room officer electronically opens the gate of a secured entrance called the Sally Port. The police car enters, stops to let the electronic gate close, and the juvenile exits the car. The control room officer electronically slides the door open, and the newcomer steps into the entrance. The control room officer closes the

door behind them, and the door into the intake hallway opens; the new-comer soon realizes that one door must close before another opens. He is finally inside the intake portion of the detention center.

GETTING SETTLED

After an officer removes the teen's handcuffs, he must take off all jewelry, empty the contents of his pockets, and take off his shoes and belt. An officer pats down the youth and checks him with a metal detector. The officer takes notes on all the teen's general information and then takes the youth to the shower area. He gives him a towel, washcloth, and soap, and when the teen has finished showering, he gives him underwear, socks, T-shirt, sweatshirt, and sweatpants. The intake officer then takes down all other important information and records it on a computer.

Some juveniles may be uncooperative or violent when they enter the facility. A detention officer takes those youths to a padded cell where they cannot hurt themselves or others. Once they calm down, the officer releases them, and the intake procedure continues.

Now a cell is assigned and some bedding provided. There are four dormitory areas called "pods," lettered A, B, C, and D, and each pod has four or five cells. Boys and girls have separate pods. The cells are equipped with a single bunk, a desk with a stool, a toilet, and a sink. Policy states only one juvenile per cell, but if the facility is full, two youths may share a double cell.

DAILY ROUTINE

Breakfast is served at 7:00 A.M. Youths leave their cells, file through electronically secured doors separating the pods from each other and the hall, and go to the cafeteria/dining room. When breakfast is over, the youths go back to their rooms until 8:30, when school begins. Again, the youths travel through electronically secured doors to the school area.

YOUTH IN PRISON

A juvenile is assigned a cell in a detention center.

Most detention centers have a computer lab.

There are three areas in the school facility. One area has long tables where students do most of their work, another area has computers, and a third is a secured area where the teacher and teacher's assistant can be. The teacher's room has electronically secured doors to the computer side and the study side; windows allow the teachers to see the students at all times.

School runs until 3:00 P.M., with several breaks during the day. At 9:30, there is a bathroom break, and at 10:30, the students go back to their rooms for a fifteen-minute break. Lunch begins at 11:30, and after that, the students stay in their rooms until they return to school at 1:00.

After school, the teens have free time back in their assigned pods. During this time, they may watch one of the four approved TV channels as well as make collect telephone calls. The cafeteria serves supper around 4:30. Everyone takes a shower once a day, usually at 5:00 in the evening. Youths are also required to clean their cells once a day.

Meals in detention centers are usually served cafeteria style.

Canadian courts send juvenile offenders to custody centers.

SPECIAL DAYS

Wednesday is court day at Clallam County Detention Facility. Most juveniles attend a court session on center property. A detention officer places the youth in leg restraints and takes her to the slider doors going into the visitor's entrance hallway. The officer then takes the youth into a secure holding cell between the hallway and the courtroom until the judge is ready for her case. The youth then enters the courtroom for her hearing. When the hearing is over, she returns to detention.

If a newly arrested youth needs to have a hearing on any other day of the week, officials take him to the courthouse downtown. Any juvenile who is arrested on a weekend is taken to the courthouse in town the following Monday.

Only parents and legal guardians may visit juveniles at Clallam Detention Facility, but occasionally the detention manager will approve a nonfamily member. Visiting hours are always from 7:00 to 8:00 in the evening on Tuesday, Thursday, Saturday, and Sunday. Visits must only last thirty minutes, unless the visitor has traveled a long distance. There must always be appropriate language and behavior between visitors and youths, or the detention staff may end the visit. Visitors come through a special entrance, where they use an intercom to ask the attending officer to open the door. They pass through the first secure sliding door and leave their belongings in the lockers provided. They then pass through another set of sliders going into the detention area. At the last set of sliders, a detention officer meets the visitors and screens them with a metal detector. The visitor goes through several more slider doors and is finally taken into the cafeteria where their visit takes place. Officers pat down residents after each visit. A detention officer is in the cafeteria during visiting times, and the control room officer monitors the room with TV cameras and audio surveillance.

A CANADIAN JUVENILE DETENTION CENTER

Prince George Youth Custody Center (PGYCC), located in British Columbia, Canada, is a coed facility that houses thirty-six juveniles; twelve are in secure custody and twenty-four are in open custody. The twenty-four juveniles in open custody have the opportunity to participate in supervised community service.

A deputy sheriff brings juveniles to PGYCC directly from court, and an official there gives them an orientation on the procedures, rules, and regulations of the center at the time of admission. The youth goes through a medical screening, and all of her possessions are taken and stored until she goes home. The center supplies all her clothes and toiletries. Each juvenile staying longer than thirty days has a case manager who helps the residents to develop and meet goals they set for their stay. Case managers also help youths apply for transfers to open custody, early release, and temporary absences.

A DAY IN JUVENILE DETENTION

A classroom in a juvenile facility

PGYCC residents start their day at 7:30 A.M. They rise, wash up, get dressed, make their beds, and are ready for breakfast by 8:00 A.M. They must finish breakfast and then do their assigned chores by 8:50 A.M. Everyone checks a chore list each day to see what new chore he has been assigned, and everyone must clean his room every day as well.

School begins by 9:00 A.M. Lunch is from 12:00 until 1:00, followed by more classes until 3:00 P.M. The juveniles then have quiet time in their rooms for half an hour. From 3:30 to 5:00, residents choose a program in which to be involved. Supper is from 5:00 until 5:30, followed by three hours of chosen program activities. Some of the programs residents can choose from are work programs, church services, outside ball field, metal/woodwork shop, board games, hobby room, television, mov-

"The child must be placed where he will gradually be restored to the true position of childhood . . . he must in short be placed in a family. Love must lead the way; faith and obedience will follow. . . . This is the fundamental principle of all true reformatory action with the young."

—English child advocate Mary Carpenter, 1853

ies, life skills, family violence sessions, anger management, and drug and alcohol counseling. Church services are held for residents between 6:30 and 8:30 on Sunday evenings. Juveniles must be in their cells by 8:30, with lights out promptly at 10:00.

Students attend school at the center but register as students of College Heights Secondary School, School District 57, Prince George, British Colombia. The motto of the school is, "Choose to Change . . . Choose to Learn." According to the school portion of the handbook on the PGYCC Web site, "We hope to change your feelings about learning so you will not return to a life of crime." The Web site goes on to say, "There is only one thing you can control . . . yourself."

PGYCC residents may have two family visits a week. Family members wanting to visit must phone the facility before noon on the previous day before the visit to have it approved. If they want to bring children along, they have to have permission and must supervise the children the entire time. For those juveniles in the secured part of the center, visiting hours are from 6:00 to 7:00 P.M. on Monday and from 1:45 to 2:45 P.M. on Saturday. Open-custody youths may have visitors from 6:00 to 7:00 P.M. on Wednesday and 10:30 A.M. to 12:00 P.M. on Saturday. Visitors need to

A DAY IN JUVENILE DETENTION

Dormitory life often takes some adjustment.

arrive fifteen minutes before the visiting hour, and if they arrive after visiting hours have begun, they cannot come in. All visitors are searched before going into the center, and they must show some form of identification. Officials allow a hug and kiss at the beginning and end of a visit but allow no other body contact.

To juveniles who have not been used to such a structured living environment, life at a detention center can come as a shock. It can also be an opportunity to learn a skill, get an education, and get one's life together. But not all detention facilities are the same, and not all offer the same positive opportunities.

CHAPTER 5

WHAT ARE JUVENILE DETENTION CENTERS LIKE?

Meet Duane. He entered Giddings State Home and School in the state of Texas at age thirteen for committing a murder during the course of a burglary. "I was a real little jerk when I first got here. I didn't want to work the program. I was hard-headed, I felt like I was innocent and didn't deserve to be incarcerated." The *1999 Annual Report of the Coalition for Juvenile Justice* tells Duane's story:

> I don't even like to talk about the Duane I was then. I was noncaring, selfish, rude, ill mannered, and very disrespectful. I used drugs and alcohol. I had a serious anger

problem. I didn't feel guilt. I just didn't think there was hope. But it turns out that there is always hope if you're willing to work.

Duane proudly showed interviewers the shining car he helped to refinish and repaint at the school's auto body shop. "It looked horrible when it came in . . . you wouldn't recognize it as the same car." When he was in the free world, Duane did not know how to paint or weld or build. Now he has these skills under his belt.

AN EXCEPTIONAL JUVENILE JUSTICE MODEL

The grounds of Giddings are beautiful, fifty-five fenced-in acres (22.3 hectares) of leafy trees and shady pathways. The tan brick and flagstone buildings, well-stocked library, and quaint chapel make the place look like a prep school. A sophisticated welding shop and a woodworking studio give residents the opportunities to build wheelchair ramps and picnic tables. The academic center has classrooms built around a glassed-in, centralized administrative area. Everything is in place and very clean. The principal is on a first-name basis with the students.

Something is always going on at Giddings. The school was one of the first in the state to have Internet access. The youth wear khaki jeans, gray shirts, and black baseball caps as they march off to yet another activity such as vocational training, chapel, GED study, intense therapy sessions, track practice, chemical-dependence group, high school diploma classes, and living skills training where they can learn skills such as how to balance a checkbook.

When the interviewer asked Duane what helped him to change, he replied with a question: "Do you know anybody who would want to work with a bunch of murderers and rapists? You don't do you, sir? Most people, they'd be scared. But staff here, they're amazing. They want to work here." He then explained how staff come even on weekends and work

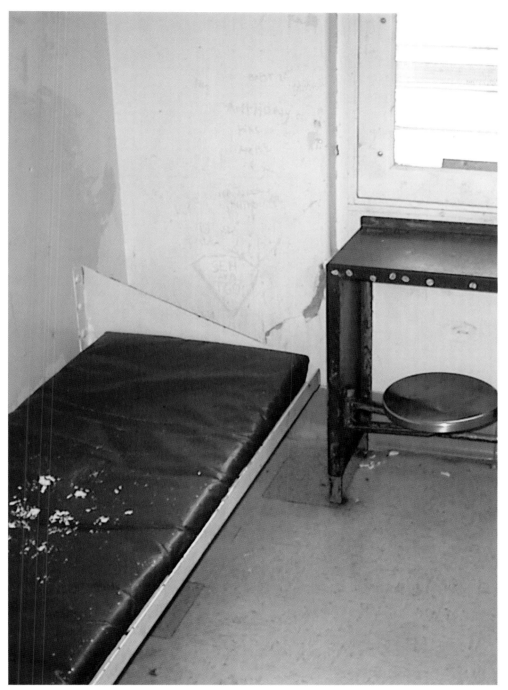

Most juvenile detention centers are cheerless places.

A cell in a juvenile facility in the United States

off-hours. The staff believed he could change—and now he has. He has made college his goal.

Some people do not like Giddings, particularly parents who have lost a child because of violence. They see the beautiful grounds, the library, and clean dorms, and they wonder why criminals should have such nice facilities. They see the classrooms that have a one-to-sixteen teacher–student ratio, they hear about the track and football teams that have won state championships, and they wonder why juvenile delinquents should have it so good. Parents also wonder why sexual offenders get up to two-and-a-half hours of therapy a day and why murderers get to spend hours

> "The most effective way to restore juvenile offenders to a law-abiding lifestyle is through healthy relationships with healthy adults in healthy environments."
>
> —Center for Research and Professional Development of the National Juvenile Detention Association

in an air-conditioned room role-playing and telling their life stories, trying to understand who they are and the crime that they committed. It's hard for these parents to care much about juvenile offenders when their own children are dead as a result of these offenders' actions.

The Victim Impact Panel at Giddings is helpful to these grieving parents as well as to the juveniles at the home. The parents tell their stories and show their children's pictures to violent juvenile offenders. The juveniles see how horrible the impact of violence is on the families of victims. The parents have the chance to grieve and feel like they are doing something constructive.

Once these grieving parents get to know what the youths at Giddings go through, most see how valuable an experience it is. Former Giddings superintendent Stan DeGerolami says that the harsh prison environment that grieving parents and tough-on-crime advocates want is actually an easy place to serve time. When authorities lock a juvenile in a cell, all he has to do is feel sorry for himself and blame someone else for his mistake. Since the kids at Giddings have to face themselves, take responsibility for their actions, and deal with the events that helped put them there, they do serve "hard" time. DeGerolami says statistics show that the reoffense rate at Giddings is extremely low; in 1998, it was 18.5 percent.

The hallway of a long-term detention center

According to DeGerolami, "Kids who successfully complete the program will not reoffend . . . the bottom line is public safety. And the public is best served by holding kids accountable and putting them through rigorous programs."

TYPES OF JUVENILE FACILITIES

According to *An Overview of Juvenile Justice* by Thomas O'Conner, great varieties of juvenile centers exist in the United States. There are long-term centers such as training schools, boot camps, ranches, forestry camps, group homes, farms, and halfway houses. Short-term facilities such as detention centers, diagnostic centers, and shelters are more common, but there are also a number of psychiatric hospitals and private juvenile detention centers. Most juvenile facilities are small, but the United States has about seventy large facilities for juveniles.

Detention centers are usually large jail-like buildings located in rural areas. They are usually short-term facilities and hold a variety of juveniles, from status offenders to those waiting for a trial. Typically, they do not have many treatment programs, but they do have educational and medical services. Studies of detention centers show they have high rates of self-destructive behaviors such as suicides, and self-mutilation.

Training schools are usually state-run facilities that are either secure or semi-secure (closed). Many times, they look like a regular high school. They usually house around fifty juveniles, although the large ones may have as many as 800. Each state has at least one maximum-security juvenile facility; there are approximately seventy such facilities in the United States, and all offer a number of treatment programs such as vocational training, counseling, GED completion (a requirement for many centers before release), and peer group activities. Most of the training schools are crowded and do not have good health care. Reports say that inmate rape and abuse are commonplace.

Foster homes, group homes, and halfway houses are the open facilities of the juvenile system. Youths usually leave during the day and must return by night. Many times officials use these homes as aftercare places. Technical violations, reoffending, and escapes are common at these homes.

The rise in the number of juvenile offenders means that more and more facilities like this must be built.

Teens in a juvenile detention center have a chance to exercise and shoot some hoops.

THE MAJORITY OF JUVENILE FACILITIES

Unfortunately, Giddings is not the norm for juvenile detention facilities. Over the last fifteen years, juvenile detention populations have risen drastically. Most youths in detention in the United States are housed in

Teen offenders' personal belongings are kept bagged until they are released.

overcrowded centers where the health standards are inadequate. Mark Soler, a youth advocate of the Youth Law Center, says that in the hurry to build more detention centers and to incarcerate more youths, such things as health care, housing, psychological services, and education are being neglected. The *1999 Annual Report of the Coalition for Juvenile Justice* quotes Soler:

> Juvenile facilities have become the dumping grounds for young people with serious mental health problems that the other agencies of government—education, health, social services—cannot or do not want to deal with. . . . the facilities do not have the professional staff or other resources to handle these people.

The executive director of the National Juvenile Detention Association, Earl Dunlap, says that the lack of good mental health programs and good education, combined with violence, crowding, and poorly paid and ill-trained staff are unfortunately the norm instead of the exception in juvenile detention centers. Overcrowding is one of the main problems. The OJJDP reported that juveniles in crowded facilities spend less time in school, have fewer family visits, are more likely to be injured, take part in fewer programs, and become ill more often.

According to the 1998 Amnesty International report "Betraying the Young," authorities are holding several thousand juveniles in adult facilities in many rural jails across the United States. Officials are mixing the juvenile population with adults, which is against international standards and federal law. Many of the adults have long criminal records and have the opportunity to attack and influence these juveniles. Soler comments that these youths are not superpredators; instead, "they are being held for traffic violations, minor property offenses, shoplifting, truancy, and running away, being beyond parental control and violating curfews."

The Amnesty International report also states that many times in juvenile facilities, staff members have harshly restrained youths and put them into prolonged isolation. This is an unusually brutal psychological punishment for a youth to endure.

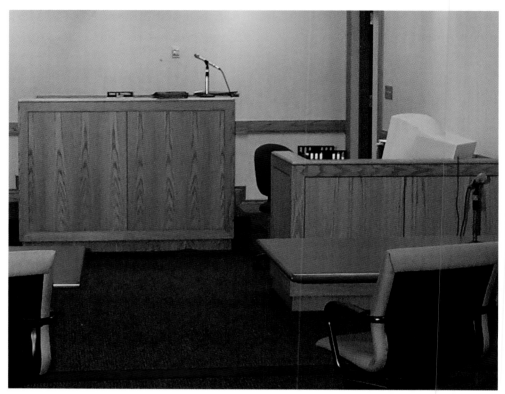
A courtroom where juvenile cases are tried

The Coalition for Juvenile Justice report finds that administrators and staff of many U.S. facilities claim they would like to improve the conditions in their detention facilities, but they lack funds and time. They are working so hard just to keep the institution's daily routine going that they hardly have the time to reflect or plan. Many of the administrators report feelings of isolation and helplessness.

Institutions can, however, change for the better. Take, for example, Ferris, the state training school in Wilmington, Delaware, which was one of the country's worst institutions. The place was so chaotic and depressing the staff would sometimes not show up for work or would quit on the spot. The American Civil Liberties Union (ACLU) filed a suit alleging that Ferris was unsanitary, overcrowded, unhealthy, and life endangering. At first, the state fought the suit, but finally it decided to work with the ACLU to better the institution. They tore down the old building and built a new one. The youth now live in light and airy rooms with large windows that look like college dorms. There is now more education than punishment, and the place is built around the new idea that isolation is easy, while confrontation is hard. The school principal, Jim Wigo, told the researchers for the Coalition for Juvenile Justice: "Ferris really is the optimal learning environment because you get 100 percent attendance. There are no drugs. Kids have to do homework. They are clean and sober and there's no negative peer pressure. They find out learning can be fun. Imagine that!" Although Ferris is not free from problems, it has made great strides in becoming more successful in rehabilitating the youth who come through its program.

CHAPTER 6

GIRLS, BOYS, AND INCARCERATION

Michelle spoke out loud for the first time in two and a half years when she cursed at a judge. She was fifteen years old and had been in thirty foster homes. The first time she stole was to get a lock to put on her door to keep her brother from sexually molesting her. Authorities put her into Minnesota's juvenile justice system. There she finally got the help she needed. The *Christian Science Monitor* Web site tells the story of how officials then sent Michelle to St. Croix girls' camp, one of the first juvenile centers in the country to have in place a "gender-specific" approach—a specific program made for girls. This was the first time she ever had choices in her life. Until then,

she was told where to go, when to go, and what to do when she got there.

Michelle and ten other girls lived in a cabin in the woods. The goal of the camp was to help the girls build trusting relationships with the staff and their peers and to build self-esteem. Together, they went through survival training, rock climbing, camping in the woods, and learned to talk about their feelings. "I always thought it was just branded on my forehead, the rapes and the abuse," Michelle said. "But when the focus quit being on what happened to me, and the focus was on me as a female, me as a girl, me as a kid, I began to get better."

WHY DO GIRLS NEED PROGRAMS DESIGNED FOR THEM?

The OJJD broadcast a program in 1999 titled "What About Girls? Females and the Juvenile Justice System," which highlighted the fact that girls and boys have different developmental issues in their teen years. Delinquent girls face many challenges while growing up, and these challenges differ from those faced by boys. Girls' needs and challenges include:

- a safe environment for healthy physical development (Instead, many are faced with violence, poverty, poor health care and nutrition, alcohol and drug abuse, and homelessness.)

- good female role models in order to develop into a healthy woman (Instead, they often experience little community support and are given **homophobic**, racist, and sexist messages.)

- feelings of competence, worth, and belonging (Most, however, encounter failure in school, low self-esteem, bad peer influences, and weak family attachments.)

- love, trust, respect, and support from adults who care in order to form good relationships and to have a healthy emotional development (Many come from dysfunctional families, where parents may have abandoned them and communication is poor or non-existent.)

- safety to explore sexuality at own pace for a healthy sexual development (Instead, they are faced with negative views of female sexuality, sexual abuse, and exploitation.)

The broadcast brought out that there are factors that increase the chances of a girl becoming a delinquent, including poor school achievement, alcohol and drug abuse, teen pregnancy, unmet mental health needs, gang membership, alternative lifestyle (lesbian activity), and the beginning of early puberty. These factors hardly ever occur by themselves; they are usually interconnected, one triggering another.

Delinquent girls face different challenges than boys.

The Corrections Canada Web site cites a study done by its group on the risk factors of female and male delinquents—the characteristics that influence a person to become a delinquent. For girls, the most important risk factors from most to least important were antisocial attitudes or friends, misbehavior or temperament problems, difficulties in school, poor relationship with parents, and minor personality issues. The pattern was the same for males, so there seemed to be no difference in risk factors between boys and girls.

Teen years are the time when boys and girls are developing their sense of gender identity—who they are as a male or female. Gender-

Friendships are important in the lives of young women.

Girls need relationships with older women.

specific programming helps girls develop their female identities in a positive way. These programs also help girls learn decision-making and life skills. They boost their confidence and give them skills that help them to get back on the right track to success.

Carol Gilligan of the Harvard Graduate School of Education has studied just how important relationships are in the life of teen girls. Although a juvenile girl is learning to separate from her parents, she needs lasting relationships with adult females. A counselor, parent, probation officer, teacher, or other adult who shows the teen she cares and is committed to her can play an important part in a girl's life. Without this close relationship, the girl may have delays in her growing-up process. She will be more likely to listen to her peers and turn to them for support instead.

Crime is rising among girls.

Minnesota is one of the national leaders in raising awareness and meeting the needs of female juvenile offenders. It was one of the first states to require that female and male juveniles receive equal service.

PROGRAMS FOR GIRLS

Because of the rise in crime among girls, a number of agencies have joined together to form the Federal Working Group on Gender Issues. They have studied programs that are effective for females and have developed strategies to help these young girls. Programs for female delinquents that are effective work with girls in a variety of ways and in different settings, and use a broad approach based in the experiences of girls.

Just as girls have many complicated problems, the answers to those problems are also complex. The girls work on behavior as it comes up in the program. The staff helps girls to see what risk factors have helped to shape them the way they are. A good program helps girls face their individual needs and helps them deal with the problems that arise with family, friends, and society.

San Francisco's SAGE (Standing Against Global Exploitation) is one program where the police or the courts refer juvenile girls for fifteen weeks. The program, designed especially for prostitutes, teaches girls how to work through issues of self-esteem, survival, and psychological and physical health. The workers help the girls with housing and teach them how to manage finances. The girls also receive job training.

Girls are more apt to commit status offenses—alcohol possession, truancy, running away, and being incorrigible—than boys are.

In 1999, about a dozen facilities in the United States offered special programs for girls. According to the *Christian Science Monitor* Web site, all the centers focus on developing good self-esteem and healthy ***mentoring*** relationships with the girls. At the same time, each center has different emphases.

The Harriet Tubman Residential Center in Auburn, New York, emphasizes the historic successes of women. When a girl walks through the entrance, she sees a wall dedicated to famous women and their accomplishments. The director, Ines Nieves-Evans, wants girls to see that women can accomplish important things. She creates an environment where girls can feel good about themselves.

Florida's PACE center is another model program. Here the staff and clients spend time celebrating girlhood. The girls follow a strict educational program but also do fun kid things like blow bubbles and play "Red Rover"—things that most kids grow up doing. Many of these girls have not experienced a normal childhood because of various factors, including sexual molestation or a parent who abused alcohol and drugs. Often the people in charge of juvenile delinquents focus on their arrest charges, their files, what they have done wrong. They forget that they have lost the experience of just being kids. PACE tries to restore this experience for the girls in their facility.

CRIMES COMMITTED BY GIRLS

Juvenile crime in general has been decreasing since 1994, but the arrest and incarceration of girls has increased. In 1999, according to a report issued by the American Bar Association and the National Bar Association, officials arrested 670,800 girls under the age of eighteen. The associations believe that the increase of arrests is due to a change in the justice system and not necessarily because of a rise in crime committed by girls.

In the 1990s, the arrest of young females on drug charges and curfew/loitering violations more than doubled. Aggravated assaults were up by 50 percent, and simple assaults almost doubled. According to the OJJDP, most of the crimes women commit are related to drug and alcohol abuse, and simple assault.

Girls in Canada and the United States are more likely to commit status offenses than are boys. These include alcohol possession, truancy, running away from home, and being "unmanageable" or "*incorrigible*." Meda Chesney-Lind and Randall G. Shelden, the authors of *Girls, Delinquency, and Juvenile Justice*, think that parents tend to want to control girls' behavior more than that of boys, causing this offense to be more common among girls. There also seems to be a bias against girls involving status offenses; studies show that boys commit these crimes as often as girls do, but authorities do not arrest boys as often.

Young girls who repeatedly commit status offenses are often trying to get away from physical and sexual abuse in the home. Once they have run away and are living on the streets, they often get into prostitution, and once a girl has become a prostitute, her abuse continues from customers and pimps.

The most common property offense among girls is shoplifting. Chesney-Lind and Shelden write that studies on this topic are few, but they show that boys will shoplift as often as girls, yet girls are more likely to get caught, reported to the police, and sent to court. The items girls steal are usually worth less than what boys steal; girls commonly steal personal items such as clothes and jewelry in the hopes of fitting in better at school. Coming from poor families, they cannot afford many luxuries.

Some girls become involved in delinquent gang activity but not at a rate higher than boys do. Girls are in gangs for the same reasons as boys: recognition, protection, and status.

More than 45 percent of all female juvenile offenders have experienced physical abuse.

"Girls in the juvenile justice system have been and are survivors as well as victims. Forced to cope with daunting and shocking conditions, they manage accommodations at tremendous cost to themselves. Their behaviors may puzzle us until we understand their predicaments. Their delinquencies are, in fact, attempts to pull themselves out of their dismal circumstances."

—Meda Chesney-Lind and Randall G. Shelden, *Girls, Delinquency, and Juvenile Justice*

CRIMINALS OR VICTIMS?

Michelle from the story that opened this chapter is an example of an average female juvenile offender in the United States. According to the *Christian Science Monitor*, 70 percent of these females have been sexually abused, although some detention centers report numbers as high as 90 percent. About 70 percent come from broken families. A study done by the National Council on Crime and Delinquency (NCCD) found that 91 percent of female juvenile offenders have failed a grade or two in school, and 58 percent have witnessed violence between parents or caregivers. More than 45 percent have been burned or beaten, and at least 25 percent have been shot or stabbed at least once. Leslie Acoca, of the NCCD in San Francisco, says, "It is very important to understand the extent to which they are not just perpetrators, but are also seriously wounded themselves."

Sexual abuse can lead to a girl running away—which in turn, can lead to her turning to prostitution and other criminal activities.

The National Justice Institute, in a study published in 2000, found a definite link between girls who have been abused and criminal behavior: 75 to 95 percent of girls in the justice system have experienced some sort of abuse. Girls are three times as likely to have been sexually abused as boys, and usually the abuse comes from family members or trusted family friends. Sexual abuse can have a terrible effect on young girls; they often feel very little self-worth, lose their ability to trust, fail in school, experience eating disorders, and may become pregnant. They are likely to commit crimes and end up in juvenile facilities.

The Web site of Juvenile Justice FYI gives a scenario with an important question to consider. A young girl may run away from home because a parent is sexually abusing her. She does not ask for government aid because she is afraid she will be sent back home to the abuser. She runs out of money soon, so she starts stealing. Later, she finds that she can make the most money by being a prostitute; she may get involved in drugs and authorities arrest her. How is the court supposed to treat such a person?

She has committed the crimes of illegal drug use, theft, and prostitution. She was also the victim of damaging abuse. Juvenile courts are determined to help these girls.

Authorities gave Michelle the chance to be a kid again at St. Croix Girls' Camp. After she left the camp, she went on to a more intensive treatment center where counselors helped her to deal with her childhood scars. At this center, Michelle celebrated her birthday and holidays for the first time in her life. She felt as though the staff let her go back and begin all over again. As of 1999, she was a mother of two, an owner of a business with thirty-two employees, and was finishing her doctorate in speech pathology. Michelle had begun to speak at conferences around the country, telling of the need for gender-specific correctional facilities. She firmly believes that girls need special juvenile detention facilities.

Regardless of gender, each teen who spends time in a detention center is affected by the experience. Those effects will influence the teen—for the better or worse—for the rest of his or her life.

CHAPTER 7

THE EFFECTS OF INCARCERATION ON YOUTH: WHAT HAPPENS AFTER?

The boy had a difficult time fitting into his foster-home placement. He was used to harsh penalties for not following rules at the juvenile facility, and the rules and consequences for not following them at his foster home were much lighter. He was having a hard time adjusting at school as well. The way he looked at it, no one was threatening to hurt him, so why should he do anything? When no one seemed to like him, he hid his emotions. Nothing made sense to him. Besides, he didn't really care what anyone thought.

Before long he ended up back in a juvenile facility. In a way, he felt relieved. At least here he knew how things worked.

EMOTIONS, ROLE MODELS, AND ROUTINES

Studies of the effects of incarceration on juveniles are almost nonexistent, but author Susan Kilbourne has recorded some observations from social workers and a psychologist who works with the National Youth Advocate Program in her book, *Children Behind Bars: Youth Who Are Detained, Incarcerated and Executed*. The number-one noticeable effect of imprisonment on juveniles is that they are less able to show emotions. A former probation officer, Wendie Parsons-Nuhn, observed that youths

Young people who have spent a lot of time in institutional settings may actually feel relieved to be arrested again—and sent back to something familiar.

Youths who have been in detention centers quickly learn not to show their emotions.

Juvenile offenders often become adult offenders.

who have been in detention centers learn not to show their emotions because they need to look strong to others around them. If they seem weak or vulnerable, someone might hurt them or take advantage of them. They get so used to hiding their emotions, and when the system releases them, they are emotionally hardened.

Another effect of incarceration is the lack of good role models. During adolescence, teens are usually busy experimenting with issues of who they are. They are learning to know themselves and show others who they are. The people they see around them influence them. In detention centers, they do not have normal successful role models around them; instead, they see mostly bad examples.

The incarceration experience is very structured and full of routine. When juveniles get out, they sometimes have a difficult time making decisions, since juvenile officers have made all of their decisions for them. David Lowenstein, a psychologist, explains in *Children Behind Bars* that the teen years are a time for psychological changes and new development. These need to happen so that the teen can be ready to leave the family and become a self-sufficient adult. It is a time for trying new roles and determining identity. Adolescents who spend time in detention centers cannot make many of their own choices, and as a result, can have a hard time learning to be independent. They often become psychologically and emotionally unstable. They do not learn good ways to deal with the future or learn decision-making skills, since they do not have a chance to make trial-and-error decisions.

Unfortunately, juveniles in detention learn other skills—skills they do not need in the outside world, but that are hard to shake off once they are learned. Juveniles have to learn to survive in detention centers. They learn from each other about different and new ways of committing crimes. Brenda Harris, an advocate with the West Virginia Youth Advocate Program, reports that many incarcerated children come out ready for adult crime. It's almost like they have a career; it's a behavior they've learned.

Violence is common at juvenile facilities. Many of the youths have come from families where violence is also common. In juvenile detention, they experience more violence, which cements it as a common

Violence may become a way of life for juvenile offenders.

"We don't need more bricks and mortar. What we do need is more social workers, more counselors, and more teachers who can work one-on-one with kids to help them deal with all the garbage, because by the time they get there [to secure facilities] they are dealing with 14 or 15 years of crap in their lives. They need to have someone who is trained to help them process that and help them see to the other side."

—Judge Yvette McGee Brown, quoted in *Children Behind Bars: Youth Who Are Detained, Incarcerated and Executed* by Susan Kilbourne

action in their lives. Lawrence Duru, a house supervisor of the Ohio Youth Advocate Program, writes: "They are no longer scared of the idea of prison, or any kind of authority. . . . But they are angry. Their underlying problems many times are never addressed. These children believe that violence is the only means they have for expression."

"NO ONE UNDERSTANDS HOW HARD IT IS OUT THERE"

Manny was a teen in the Arizona model juvenile detention program described by authors Bortner and Williams. The program was very effective for him; he did well and was intent on changing his life when the program released him. After his release, he enrolled in a community college close to his home, but he found it difficult to get away from old friends

Breaking away from a gang takes courage.

and gang members. Rival gang members jumped him one day in front of a local market, and he became afraid to spend any time with his girlfriend and their baby for fear he could put them in danger. At his home, he was afraid that his younger brothers and sisters would become victims of a drive-by shooting. (The house already had bullet holes from previous shootings.) His fear was immense. All he could think was: *I don't want to be the next victim, I just don't want to be the next victim.* Ten months after his release, two young men came to the house and asked for Manny by name. When he came to the door, they shot him and his stepfather. The stepfather died immediately; Manny died three hours later at the hospital.

When juveniles leave incarceration facilities, like Manny, they return to the homes in neighborhoods where they previously got into trouble. The circumstances and people that influenced them years ago are most likely still there. For many, influences outside the prison are daunting. Both the youths that returned to their homes and those who went to residential facilities found this to be true. Violence usually saturates the environment, and old enemies do not forget past grudges.

Charles was optimistic about his release from detention. He believed he could stay away from trouble with the law and control his drinking. He did not think he would be back. Before he left the center, he told his counselors he thought there was little anyone could do to change the violence in his neighborhood. "[Staff members] can't do nothing for me. . . . I'm just gonna go—you know, I'm gonna go with the flow, do what needs to be done, and stay out of trouble. It's as simple as that." Unfortunately, Charles was back into drinking three weeks after his release. Four months later, officials arrested him for killing two men in different armed robberies. One of Charles's problems was that he had a great attraction to guns, and they were easily accessible: "Once you touch it . . . the bigger the gun, the bigger you feel. . . . It's like nobody else out there has a gun."

After authorities arrested Charles and returned him to juvenile detention, he told the authors of *Youth in Prison*, "I really thought that I was rehabilitated, but no one understands how hard it is out there. . . . It would have broken me down to see all those staff who believed in me."

When the juvenile system releases youths back to their communities, the teens face the realities of their existence. Most of them are poor, come from dysfunctional or violent families, and have drugs and gang activity at their fingertips. It is hard to find jobs when employers have applications from other youths whom have never been in trouble with the law. Often these ex-offenders receive no support in their efforts to get more education. When the youths involved in the model program described in *Youth in Prison* left detention, several were very enthusiastic about getting a higher education. But when faced with "tedious, demanding requirements and persistent failure," they quickly became discouraged.

Darnell was one of these youths. He was soft spoken and gentle, of average intelligence with good leadership qualities. When officials arrested him for simple assault, it was a real blow to his self-concept. By the time he left the program, he was reassured of his worth and was encouraged about his future. He enthusiastically enrolled in a community college. Unfortunately, the school counselor did not advise him to take it easy his first semester, and he signed up for a full course load. During his

Helping incarcerated youth helps our entire society.

first few weeks, he was overwhelmed with all the work involved. Darnell became so discouraged that he left the college and disappeared for four days. When he came home, he refused to go back to school. He had only been out of prison for two months, and he was already discouraged and depressed. Authors Bortner and Williams write, "Darnell said that when he was sentenced to prison he had questioned his value as a human being. After he 'failed' at the community college he was certain he would never amount to anything."

Juvenile facilities cannot simply release youths and expect them to survive successfully in the same environment from which they came. If the institution has been a healthy, nurturing place, they have helped to set the juvenile on the right track—but the youth needs follow-up care to stay on that track.

In the past century, the juvenile justice system has come a long way in both Canada and the United States. Many improvements have been made over the years—but more improvements need to be made.

The U.S. 1999 Annual Report of the Coalition for Juvenile Justice ends their report by saying that all youth in detention need to live in a humane, safe, and rehabilitative environment. Everyone—including the government, youth workers, the media, the juvenile court, and the public—needs to work together to accomplish this. The public must come to understand that giving incarcerated youth better conditions to live in will help us all have a healthier, safer society.

GLOSSARY

Aboriginal: Having to do with Canada's Native population.

adjudicated: Made a legal decision.

apprentices: Young people legally bound to serve an artisan or other experienced adult worker for a prescribed period with a view to learning an art or trade.

arson: The willful and malicious burning of property.

benevolent: Showing kindness or goodwill.

community service: Specific actions that benefit the larger community in some way, usually assigned in place of some other punishment.

extenuating: Diminishing the seriousness of something.

extrajudicial: Outside normal legal proceedings.

felonies: Serious crimes for which the punishment is usually imprisonment for more than a year or death.

gang-banger: Member of a violent street gang.

halfway house: A residence for individuals after release from institutionalization (as for mental disorder, drug addiction, or criminal activity) that is designed to facilitate their readjustment to private life.

homophobic: Irrational fear of, aversion to, or discrimination against homosexuality or homosexuals.

incorrigible: Impossible to correct or reform.

infamous: Famous for something bad.

infanticides: Murders of babies.

larceny: The unlawful taking of personal property from another.

majority: The age of legal responsibility.

mentoring: Acting as a positive role model.

misdemeanors: Crimes that are less serious than felonies.

moralistic: Concerned with narrow and often rigid interpretations of right and wrong.

parole: A conditional release of a prisoner serving an indeterminate or unexpired sentence.

philanthropist: Someone who desires to improve the welfare of humanity, especially through charitable activities.

posttraumatic stress disorder: A psychiatric disorder that can occur following the experience of a life-threatening event. People who suffer from this disorder often relive the experience through nightmares and flashbacks, have difficulty sleeping, and feel detached or estranged; these symptoms can be severe enough and last long enough to significantly impair the person's daily life.

probation: The action of suspending the sentence of a convicted offender and giving the offender freedom during good behavior under the supervision of a probation officer.

Quaker: A member of a Christian group that stresses Inner Light (interior divine insights), rejects sacraments and an ordained ministry, and opposes war; Quakers are also called Friends.

rehabilitation: To restore or bring to a condition of health or useful and constructive activity.

restitution: The act of making good or giving an equivalent for some injury.

self-incrimination: The act of offering evidence or statements that would prove one's own guilt.

stigmatize: Label as socially undesirable.

survivor guilt: Sense of remorse often felt by a survivor of an incident that claimed the lives of others.

vagrancy: The state of wandering with no permanent place to live.

wayward: Characterized by willfulness or disobedience.

FURTHER READING

Bortner, M.A., and Linda M. Williams. *Youth in Prison*. New York: Routledge, 2000.

Bridges, George S., Joseph G. Weis, and Robert D. Crutchfield. *Juvenile Delinquency Readings*. Thousand Oaks, Calif.: Pine Forge Press, 2001.

Coalition for Juvenile Justice. *Ain't No Place Anybody Would Want To Be: Conditions of Confinement for Youth: 1999 Annual Report*. Washington, D.C.: Coalition for Juvenile Justice, 1999.

Edgar, Kathleen. *Youth Violence, Crime, and Gangs: Children at Risk*. Farmington Hills, Mich.: Gale, 2004.

Ferro, Jeffrey. *Crime: A Serious American Problem*. Farmington Hills, Mich.: Gale, 2003.

Hjelmeland, Andy. *Prisons: Inside the Big House (Pro/Con)*. Minneapolis, Minn.: Lerner Publications, 1996.

Kilbourne, Susan. *Children Behind Bars: Youth Who Are Detained, Incarcerated and Executed*. Washington, D.C.: Youth Advocate Program International, 1999.

Laci, Miklos. *Prisons and Jails: A Deterrent to Crime?* Farmington Hills, Mich.: Gale, 2004.

YOUTH IN PRISON

FOR MORE INFORMATION

Church Council on Justice and Corrections
www.ccjc.ca/currentissues/bootcamp.cfm

CNN.com Law Center
archives.cnn.com/2001/LAW/04/30/girls.crime.study/index.html

Department of Justice Canada
canada.justice.gc.ca/en/ps/inter/juv_jus_min/sec01a.html

Department of Justice Canada
www.justice.gc.ca/en/ps/yj/information/factsheet_vic1.html

Female Juvenile Delinquents
ojjdp.ncjrs.org/pubs/principles/ch1_4.html

Juvenile Justice FYI
www.juvenilejusticefyi.com/history_of_juvenile_justice.html

Prince George Youth Correctional Centre
www.canadiancontent.net/en/jd/go?Url=http://members.pgonline.com/~pgycc

Public Safety and Emergency Preparedness Canada
www.prevention.gc.ca/en/library/publications/children/profiles/#young

Second Chances
www.canadiancontent.net/en/jd/go?Url=http://www.cjcj.org/centennial

Standing Against Global Exploitation/The SAGE Project
www.sageprojectinc.org

Statistics Canada
142.206.72.67/04/04b/04b_002b_e.htm

Publisher's note:
The Web sites listed on this page were active at the time of publication. The publisher is not responsible for Web sites that have changed their addresses or discontinued operation since the date of publication. The publisher will review and update the Web-site list upon each reprint.

BIBLIOGRAPHY

"An Overview of Juvenile Justice." http://faculty.ncwc.edu/toconnor/111/111lect14.htm.

Austin, James, and John Irwin. *It's About Time: America's Imprisonment Binge*. Belmont, Calif.: Wadsworth, 1994.

Bortner, M. A., and Linda M. Williams. *Youth in Prison*. New York: Routledge, 1997.

Canadian Center for Adolescent Research. http://ccar.briercrest.ca/stats/crime.shtml#statcan.

Christian History Institute. "Why Mrs. Fry Willingly Went to Prison." http://chi.gospelcom.net/GLIMPSEF/Glimpses/glmps090.shtml.

Coalition for Juvenile Justice. *Ain't No Place Anybody Would Want To Be: Conditions of Confinement for Youth: 1999 Annual Report*. Washington, D.C.: Coalition for Juvenile Justice, 1999.

Department of Justice Canada. "The Evolution of Juvenile Justice in Canada." http://canada.justice.gc.ca/en/ps/inter/juv_jus_min/sec01a.html.

Department of Justice Canada. http://www.justice.gc.ca.

Edgar, Kathleen. *Youth Violence, Crime, and Gangs: Children at Risk*. Farmington Hills, Mich.: Gale, 2004.

Female juvenile delinquents. http://ojjdp.ncjrs.org/pubs/principles/ch1_4.html.

Ferro, Jeffrey. *Crime: A Serious American Problem*. Farmington Hills, Mich.: Gale, 2003.

Find Law for the Public. "The Juvenile Justice System." http://criminal.findlaw.com/crimes/criminal_stages/criminal_juvenile_justice(1).html.

Hjelmeland, Andy. *Prisons: Inside the Big House (Pro/Con)*. Minneapolis, Minn.: Lerner Publications, 1996.

Justice Studies—North Carolina University. "Juvenile Offenders and Troubled Teens." http://faculty.ncwc.edu/toconnor/juvjusp.htm.

Juvenile Justice FYI. "History of U.S. Juvenile Justice System." http://www.juvenilejusticefyi.com/history_of_juvenile_justice.html.

"Juvenile Justice Not so Equal for Girls." *Christian Science Monitor*. http://csmonitor.com/cgi-bin/durableRedirect.pl?/durable/1999/02/16/p1s2.htm.

Kilbourne, Susan. *Children Behind Bars: Youth Who Are Detained, Incarcerated and Executed*. Washington, D.C.: YAP International, 1999.

Laci, Miklos. *Prisons and Jails: A Deterrent to Crime?* Farmington Hills, Mich.: Gale, 2004.

Prince George Youth Custody Centre. http://www.canadiancontent.net/en/jd/go?Url=http://members.pgonline.com/~pgycc.

Public Safety and Emergency Preparedness Canada. http://www.prevention.gc.ca/en/library/publications/children/profiles/#young.

Second Chances. http://www.canadiancontent.net/en/jd/go?Url=http://www.cjcj.org/centennial.

"What About Girls? Females and the Juvenile Justice System." http://www.juvenilenet.org/jjtap/archives/girlsconf/partic.pdf.

YOUTH IN PRISON

INDEX

PICTURE CREDITS

British Library: p. 11
iStock: p. 49
    Alex Hinds: p. 50
    Anita Patterson: p. 86
    Dan Brandenburg: p. 38
    David Grady: p. 100
    Eva Serrabass: p. 102
    Frances Twitty: p. 96
    Greg Nicholas: p. 31
    Jacob Jensen: p. 98
    Jan Ball: p. 40
    Jeff McDonald: p. 55
    Joseph Jean Rolland
     Dubé: p. 81
    Justin Griffith: p. 26
    Kelly Cline: p. 57
    Linda Shannon: p. 94
    Marie Cloke: p. 28
    Nuno Silva: pp. 32, 37, 48
    Oleksandr Gumerov: p. 43
    Pavel Pospisil: p. 84
    Robert Deal: p. 83
    Rose Hayes: p. 42
    Sharon Dominick: p. 56

Tiffany Ring: p. 46
Tobias Ott: p. 90
Jupiter Images: pp. 58, 62, 82, 88, 95
Lancaster County Government: pp. 67, 70
LawforKids.com: p. 74
Monroe County Library System: pp. 12, 13
Nova Scotia Archives and Records Administration: p. 14
Sandusky County Juvenile Detention Center: p. 72
Wood County Court: pp. 60, 68, 76

To the best knowledge of the publisher, all other images are in the public domain. If any image has been inadvertently uncredited, please notify Harding House Publishing Service, Vestal, New York 13850, so that rectification can be made for future printings.

Chapter opening art was taken from a painting titled *Neighborhood Institution* by Raymond Gray.

Raymond Gray has been incarcerated since 1973. Mr. Gray has learned from life, and hard times, and even from love. His artwork reflects all of these.

BIOGRAPHIES

AUTHOR

Roger Smith holds a degree in English education and formerly taught in the Los Angeles public schools. Smith did volunteer work with youthful inmates at a juvenile detention facility in Los Angeles. He currently lives in Arizona.

SERIES CONSULTANT

Dr. Larry E. Sullivan is Associate Dean and Chief Librarian at the John Jay College of Criminal Justice and Professor of Criminal Justice in the doctoral program at the Graduate School and University Center of the City University of New York. He first became involved in the criminal justice system when he worked at the Maryland Penitentiary in Baltimore in the late 1970s. That experience prompted him to write the book *The Prison Reform Movement: Forlorn Hope* (1990; revised edition 2002). His most recent publication is the three-volume *Encyclopedia of Law Enforcement* (2005). He has served on a number of editorial boards, including the *Encyclopedia of Crime and Punishment,* and *Handbook of Transnational Crime and Justice.* At John Jay College, in addition to directing the largest and best criminal justice library in the world, he teaches graduate and doctoral level courses in criminology and corrections. John Jay is the only liberal arts college with a criminal justice focus in the United States. Internationally recognized as a leader in criminal justice education and research, John Jay is also a major training facility for local, state, and federal law enforcement personnel.